JUDE DA[...] an internationally renowned author and illustrator, whose books for
Frances L[...] include *The Gift of the Sun*, *The Dove*, *To Everything There is a Season*,
Let Th[...] Peace, *The Faraway Island*, *Sivu's Six Wishes* and *Thank You, Jackson*,
which her [...] and Niki Daly wrote for her to illustrate. Jude and Niki Daly live in the
little seaside town of Kleinmond, South Africa.

NIKI DALY h[...] numerous awards at home and abroad for his lyrical writing and lively
illustration[...] *So Fast, Songololo*, winner of The Katrine Harries Award and a US Parent's
Choice Awar[...] the way for post-apartheid South African children's books, and, with
*Fly, Eagle, F*[...] one of the Top Fifty Diversity Titles, sponsored by Seven Stories, National
Centre for Ch[...] s Books, in 2014. *Jamela's Dress*, first in the bestselling *Jamela* series, was
another mile[...] book, winning the Children's Literature Choice Award, the Parent's Choice
Award and the[...] Pan Silver Award in Sweden. Niki's recent books for Frances Lincoln include
*The Herd Boy*[...] *No More Kisses for Bernard*. In 2009 Niki Daly was awarded the Molteno Gold
Meda[...] major contribution towards South African children's literature.

For Seb and Hamish

JANETTA OTTER-BARRY BOOKS

Text copyright © Jude Daly 2014
Illustrations copyright © Niki Daly 2014

The rights of Jude Daly and Niki Daly to be identified as the author and illustrator of this work
have been asserted by them in accordance with the Copyright, Designs and Patents Act, 1988 (United Kingdom).

First published in Great Britain and in the USA in 2014 by
Frances Lincoln Children's Books, 74–77 White Lion Street, London N1 4PF
www.franceslincoln.com

This paperback edition first published in Great Britain and in the USA in 2015

A catalogue record for this book is available from the British Library.

ISBN 978-1-84780-602-4
Set in KosmikPlainOne
Printed in China
1 3 5 7 9 8 6 4 2

# Seb and Hamish

Written by Jude Daly
Illustrated by Niki Daly

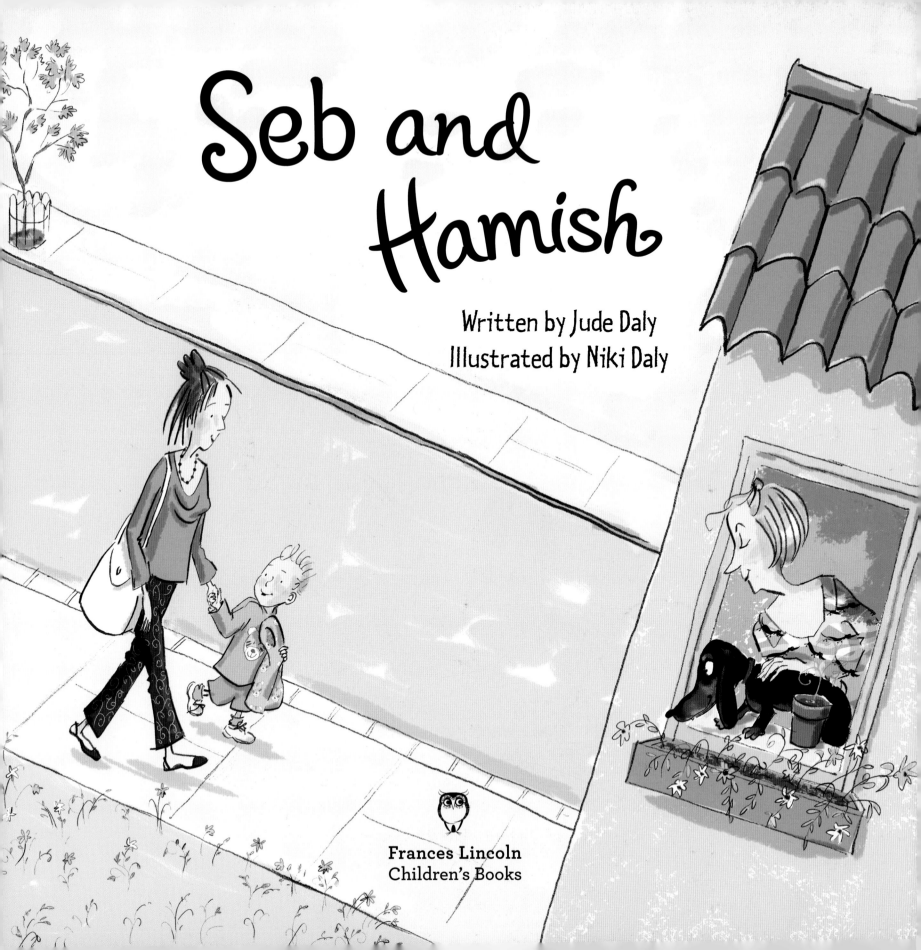

Frances Lincoln
Children's Books

Seb and Mama were going to visit
their new neighbour, Mrs Kenny.
Seb was looking very smart in his tiger top.
Mama was looking very smart too.

Mama lifted Seb up to ring the bell.

Inside, Mrs Kenny was busy putting
smiley faces on some cookies.
Seb rang the bell again.

Hamish rushed to the door.

Woof! Woof! Woof! Woof!

Woof-woof!
Woof-woof!

Seb covered his ears
and hid behind Mama.

# Woof-woof! Woof-woof!

He grabbed Mama's hand
and pulled her away from
the door. Then in a tiny
little voice he said,
"Home."

Mrs Kenny opened the front door.
She was smiling, and holding
Hamish in her arms.
"Hello, Tiger," said Mrs Kenny.
"Woof!" went Hamish.
"Up," said Seb in his tiny voice.

Woof-woof, woof, woof!

Mama picked Seb up.

"Hamish is just saying hello," she said.

Seb's lip trembled.

He shrank into his top

like a tortoise into its shell.

Woof-woof, woof-woof!

"Oh, dearie me," said Mrs Kenny.

"He's just SO excited to meet you."

Woof-woof, woof-woof!

"Home," whispered Seb.

Mrs Kenny put Hamish into her bedroom and closed the door. Seb checked the door to make sure it was properly shut.

In the kitchen, Seb saw
Mrs Kenny's toys and forgot
all about Hamish.
He wrapped his blankey around
a teddy and put it in the train
with his juice and some
smiley faces.

Clickety-clack, clickety-clack!

Choo-choo!

The train went through Mama's legs,
under the table and round Mrs Kenny's chair.

It went down the passage.

# Clickety-clack, Clickety-clack.

Then it stopped for a tea break.

While Seb was eating a smiley face,
the nose fell off and disappeared
under Mrs Kenny's bedroom door.

Seb poked his finger under the door.
Something gave it a soft lick.

And when Seb looked through the gap, two bright eyes looked back at him.

"Hello," said Seb.

*Sniff-sniff, sniff-sniff.*

"Hello, Hamish," said Seb.

*Sniff-sniff, sniff-sniff.*

Ever so slowly, Seb opened the door
and peeped through. Hamish's tail
was wagging so much it made his
bottom wiggle-waggle.
"Funny Hamish," said Seb.

Seb touched Hamish's smooth
silky head. He felt a floppy ear.
He stroked it and he stroked it.

It was even softer than his blankey.

Mama and Mrs Kenny had been chattering away like
two busy birds when Mrs Kenny said,
"Time to check up on the train driver!"

So Mama and Mrs Kenny tiptoed down the passage . . .

and there they found Seb.

He was fast asleep –
with his new best friend.

# More great read-aloud picture books by Jude and Niki Daly
# Published by Frances Lincoln Children's Books

978-1-84780-428-0

### No More Kisses for Bernard
Written and illustrated by Niki Daly

Everyone loves Bernard! Especially his four 'kissy' aunts who plaster him with  squeaky-sweet-hello kisses, lipsticky-pink-and-glow kisses, sneaky-on-the-nose kisses and smooch-got-to-go kisses. How much more can a boy take?

"A delight" – *Publishers Weekly*

"Wittily illustrated, this is a story for everyone"
– *Independent on Sunday*

978-1-84780-484-6

### Thank You, Jackson
Written by Niki Daly
Illustrated by Jude Daly

When Jackson the donkey refuses to take his load of vegetables up the hill to market, the farmer is at his wits' end. No amount of pushing, pulling or threats will make the old donkey budge – until his little boy, Goodwill, whispers a secret message in Jackson's ear. This beautiful, sun-drenched African tale, full of charm and humour, shows how saying please and thank you can make all the difference.

Frances Lincoln titles are available from all good bookshops.
You can also buy books and find out more about your favourite titles,
authors and illustrators on our website: www.franceslincoln.com